Inspiring Stories about Diversity

Empowering Tales to Teach Kids Empathy, Cultivate Kindness, Celebrate Differences, and Encourage Acceptance That All Children Belong

Lily Nicolai

CONTENTS

Introduction	V
Becky's Beautiful Braids	1
Sara's Special Signs	13
Santiago's Secret Language	21
Hasika's Henna Hands	31
Finnley's Blended Family	39
Fotina's Favorite Foods	47
Mason's Unique Mind	55
Hadia's Hijab Help	63
Minato's Mighty Music	71
Sammy's Important Saturdays	79
Skylar's Unusual Summer	87
Victor's Tasty Veggies	95
Conclusion	103

INTRODUCTION

Hi there!

Are you ready for a new kind of magic?

Yes, there are so many kinds of magic, but this one is special. It's called the *magic of diversity*.

But what is diversity, and what makes this magic so special?

Well, look around you! Diversity means the differences among people that make our world colorful and interesting.

We all have different hair and eye colors, different names, clothes, and homes. We speak different languages, eat different foods, and we like different things.

Some of us can run super fast, and some can jump super high. Some of us can sing, and some can dance! Are you beginning to see how the world is rich in diversity?

Each and every one of us is unique! There is not a single person exactly like you. Isn't that magical?!

There are so many ways that people can be different from one another, and that's why you're about to meet twelve new friends! Hasika, Linda, Becky, Santiago, and others will guide you on a magical journey to show you not only a completely new world but also how amazing our differences can be.

So, let's get started!

Clap your hands and discover a new magical world!

BECKY'S BEAUTIFUL BRAIDS

Becky couldn't wait for the summer vacation with her family! Her dad traveled a lot with his job, and she missed him so much during the school year. Summers were the best because the whole family got to go where Dad was working. And it usually meant a full two months in a new country! Yes, every new year, Becky had a new adventure!

Becky had no brothers or sisters but always met lots of friends to play with because wherever they went, Becky got to go to summer camp. *Who will I meet this time?* She wondered excitedly as she packed.

After a long plane ride and an exciting weekend exploring the sights and yummy food of the new city with her family, Becky was so ready for camp on Monday.

I'll meet so many new friends! Maybe we'll play some games I've never played before, and I can share them back home with my friends. I might learn something new about their country or taste new snacks, she wondered to herself, her happy heart beating fast.

On Sunday evening, Becky started to get ready.

"Mom, I want my braids to be extra special for meeting new friends," Becky said.

After working on her hair for an hour, her braids were ready, and finally, Becky clipped on her best bow.

"Wow! The braids look awesome! Thanks, Mom!" Becky exclaimed.

The following day, Becky arrived at camp, where she was introduced to the new kids. They played, did arts and crafts, and painted.

This is the best day ever! she thought.

But it got even better. Later that day, Becky and some girls decided to make a dance show. They designed their routine and wanted to show everyone at the camp the next day.

"Hey girls, what should we wear? We need to look the same!" said Jenna.

"Yes! We can all wear pink T-shirts, and let's put our hair in two ponytails!" said Laura.

Becky felt her tummy twist and turn. She knew her mom wouldn't do this with her hair. *I won't even bother asking her,* she thought. She did, however, put on her pink T-shirt without changing her hairstyle.

"Becky, your hair is not right!" Laura said.

"You'll ruin our show! We have to look the same!" Jenna shouted. "You can't be in the show looking like that!"

All the girls agreed that she couldn't be in the show.

Becky couldn't believe it. All because of a hairstyle! She walked away from the girls and sat by herself in a quiet corner.

"I wish I never had such thick, curly hair!" Becky mumbled.

A camp counselor noticed her sitting in the corner.

"Hey, what's wrong, Becky?" she asked

"I hate my hair!" Becky declared.

"What do you mean? You were so happy with your braids and that beautiful bow just yesterday. What changed?" the camp counselor asked.

"Why can't I have hair that goes easily into ponytails? I want to change my hairstyle every day, just like the other girls," Becky replied.

"Well, Becky, I'm sorry to hear you feel that way," the camp counselor said. "I love how your hair looks! Yes, it may look different, but it's unique and a part of you, and you should be proud of *all* of you."

"Well, I am. I mean, I was. But it means I can't do the show with the girls," Becky complained. "And we practiced so much, and it was so much fun!"

"Why not?" asked the camp counselor.

Becky explained to the counselor about the pink t-shirts and hair for the show.

"Well, do the girls understand why it's harder for you to change your hairstyle so easily?" the counselor asked.

"Well, no, I guess not...," Becky said.

"So, is there a chance they might just think you didn't want to match or didn't care to make an effort to put your hair in two ponytails?" the counselor asked.

"Um, maybe," Becky said.

"I know you are new, so sharing a bit about yourself may help. People can only make decisions based on what they think they know. By sharing, they may understand you better, especially as none of them has hair like yours," the counselor said.

"Let me have a quick chat with the girls first. Just like you are learning how to handle these situations, there are things they need to learn too."

"Hey girls," said the counselor, "I understand you are preparing a very special show for us."

"Yes! We are so excited about it!" Jenna said, "But we must change our routine now because we are down one person."

"Oh really! Why?" the counselor asked.

"It's Becky! She wants to do her own thing and not match with the group," Laura said.

"What needs matching?" the counselor asked.

"The pink T-shirts and ponytails!" Jenna said.

The counselor looked at Becky and said, "I see she's got her pink T-shirt."

"Yes, but she just ignored the ponytails!" Jenna said.

"I see that," the counselor said. "Did you ask her why?"

The girls all went silent and looked down, feeling a bit ashamed.

"No, we didn't. We just assumed she just didn't want to," Laura quietly said.

"Do you think you girls might have been too quick to make a decision without asking your friend why? Do you think you should have a chat with her now?" the counselor asked.

"Definitely," all the girls agreed.

"Hey, Becky, why didn't you make the ponytails to match us?" Jenna asked.

"Well, I couldn't," Becky said.

"But why?" Laura asked.

"It takes my mom over an hour to style my hair, and that's why I can only change my hairstyle every one to two weeks," Becky explained.

"Then why do you do the braids if it takes so long?" Laura asked.

"Well, my type of hair can more easily break or get damaged, and braids are a way to protect it so it can grow better. It's a tradition to braid our hair that's been passed down by my great-grandparents from Africa, and mostly, I like how it looks. My mom makes the best designs! But we don't restyle that often because it takes so long. Mom did my hair on Sunday, so it was just too soon to restyle it," Becky said.

"Wow... I had no idea! I'm so glad you told us," Laura said.

"Well, I'm more glad you asked," Becky replied.

"We still want you in the routine! I have an idea!" Jenna said. "How about we do our show next week! Becky, can your mom do a cute hairstyle with two ponytails then? What do you think?"

"Oh, yes! I bet she can! My mom is super creative!" Becky exclaimed.

"Deal! Next week it is!" Jenna said.

The week flew by, and soon Becky's mom had given her a new hairstyle—two long ponytails. Becky had the longest ponytails in the group! She waved her hair happily, and the girls were amazed.

"Wow! You look amazing!" Jenna exclaimed.

"Your hair is so cool!" Laura said.

The show was even better. Everyone clapped loudly along with the dance and seemed to really enjoy it.

“Group hug!” shouted the girls happily.

Two weeks later, their friend Laura returned to camp after vacation and immediately ran to Becky.

“Look, Becky! I got one braid in my hair with these super cool beads on vacation!” Laura said.

All the girls thought it was so cute, and Becky felt proud of her hair.

“Do you know that long ago, the different colored beads used in braids meant different things?” Becky said.

“Oh, really? Mine are blue; what does it mean?” Laura asked.

Becky laughed, “I have no idea. Maybe I’ll try to find out for you.”

“But for now, TAG! You’re it!” and with that, the girls ran off laughing and playing.

From that day on, Becky never wished she didn’t have African hair and wore her braids often. She was super proud of her origins and traditions.

Isn't it cool to learn new things? Our world is full of different people with different types of hair, eyes, skin colors, and shapes. Maybe you are the only one with red hair in your class, or your skin is lighter than

your neighbor's, or you know someone with the coolest eyes because one is green and one is blue. Differences in our appearances are passed down to us by our family. It's part of what makes each one of us unique and amazing!

When you see something different, why not ask about it before deciding anything? The answer will help you understand better. And sometimes, we may need to make some little changes for those differences so that everyone can fit in and have fun. Just like the girls waiting till the next week so that Becky could change her hairstyle. You could also make some changes for people's differences in other ways. You might consider making nut-free cupcakes so friends allergic to nuts can enjoy them too. Or maybe you really want pepperoni pizza, but you can all agree on cheese pizza in case some people can't eat meat. It's worth making the change to include others and see your friends happy, isn't it?

Becky wants you to remember something: it's great to learn about people's differences, especially when we meet new friends. What we learn can be interesting and quite fascinating! Also, no one wants to be left out; it's not a nice feeling at all! And if there is a way to include everyone, shouldn't we try that?

A GIFT FOR YOU

Hi there reader!

Did you enjoy the first story?
Would you like to see Becky and all the other kids in this book in a FULL-COLOR album? Scan the QR code below to download all their colorful pics.

And when you do, you will also get twelve sets of interesting and amazing facts–one set for each story! That's 120 cool facts!
These will teach you even more about that type of diversity!

So, go ahead and have your grown-up, please **scan this QR Code with a phone camera to get your color pics and fabulous bonus facts!**

https://bit.ly/DiversityGift

SARA'S SPECIAL SIGNS

Abigail was excited to go to her local park. She always was! It was the best playground around, with lots of slides, swings, and the biggest jungle gym of any playground she knew.

As her little brother played in the kiddie obstacle course, Abigail noticed a girl about her age. Abigail is a friendly girl who loves meeting new people, so she shouted from the top of the slide, "Hi, there!"

Abigail began waving her hands to get the girl's attention, but the girl didn't seem to notice her. She was too busy following a butterfly fluttering around the nearby bushes. Abigail liked the way the girl played with the butterfly and wanted to join her, so she slid down and made her way over.

Soon she stood beside the girl near the bushes. They both stared at the colorful butterfly as it landed on the water fountain.

"It's so beautiful! Look at the patterns and colors on its wings!" Abigail said cheerfully.

But the girl didn't say a word.

"Do you want to play with me?" Abigail asked as the two girls continued looking down at the butterfly.

Suddenly, the girl ran off without saying anything or even waving to Abigail!

Abigail was so disappointed.

Why won't she play with me? She wondered sadly.

"Mom! That girl over there doesn't want to play with me. She's not nice!" Abigail complained.

"How do you know that?" Mom asked.

"I asked her, and she just ran off!" Abigail said.

"Oh, Sweetie, maybe she's just shy," Mom said. "Look, she's over there with her mom. How about we both go over and say hi together?"

"No! If she doesn't want to play with me, I'm not asking again. She can play by herself. She was mean to me!" Abigail said, crossing her arms angrily.

"Oh, you can't be sure of all that. Maybe it was a misunderstanding. Let's at least try one more time," Mom said.

Abigail grumpily followed her mom. It wasn't long before the moms introduced themselves and their daughters.

"Hi, nice to meet you. This is Abigail," Abigail's mom said.

"Nice to meet you. This is Sara," said the other mom.

"Hi, Sara," said Abigail.

"Oh, Abigail," said the other mom, "Sara can't hear you."

"What do you mean? Should I speak louder?" Abigail was confused.

"No, she can't hear at all. She was born not being able to hear. That means she is deaf," Sara's mom explained.

Abigail was shocked. She looked at Sara, hiding behind her mom. Abigail felt ashamed for all the things she had thought about Sara. She had never met a person who couldn't hear, and it seemed so strange to her. A million questions ran through her head.

"So, how do you talk to her?" Abigail finally asked Sara's mom.

"We use sign language," she replied. "Here, let me show you. Use this to tell her, 'Hi, how are you?' Sara will reply to you using signs, and I'll tell you what they mean."

“Oh! Sign language?! That’s amazing!” Abigail exclaimed.

Sara’s mother showed Abigail the signs, and she carefully watched and remembered them. Abigail turned to Sara and showed her the signs.

This is so fun! thought Abigail.

Sara stepped out from behind her mom and signed the same thing back. Both girls smiled at each other.

“This is so cool! Can she speak at all?” Abigail asked.

“Well, she tries to, but it's difficult to understand her. Hearing and speech often go together. Imagine if you never heard your mom speak to you; it would be harder for you to learn how to talk. She has never heard normal sounds and speech,” Sara’s mom explained.

Abigail couldn’t imagine not hearing her mom's voice, and a piece of her felt sad inside.

“How do I ask her to play with me?” Abigail asked.

Sara’s mom showed her the signs, and again Abigail copied them. Sara’s face lit up with a bright smile.

Abigail gestured for Sara to follow her, and happily, the girls ran off playing. Not knowing any more sign language, Abigail used her hands to point at things like the slide, and Sara followed. Abigail kept looking at Sara’s face to see if she agreed with each activity.

It wasn't long before Sara began showing Abigail what games to play too.

Abigail started making different faces and other body motions to 'talk' with Sara, like flapping her wings to suggest playing with butterflies and jumping up and down to say, "Let's go on the trampoline!" The girls laughed and played and had so much fun!

After a while, the girls got tired and thirsty, so they stopped for water and a snack together. Abigail had many more questions for Sara's mom.

"How does she hear her teacher in school? How can you read stories to her?" Abigail asked.

"It takes a special teacher and a lot of patience, but bit by bit, Sara is learning more sign language and beginning to learn to read lips. It's like if you had to learn a new language but with no volume," Sara's mom said, happy that someone was so interested in her little girl.

Instead of feeling sad and sorry for Sara, Abigail began to see how brave Sara was and admired her for being so happy even though she had this challenge.

“Can I play with Sara tomorrow?” Abigail asked.

“Why don’t you ask her?” Sara’s mom said and showed her the signs.

Abigail copied the signs, and Sara replied with a big smile.

As Abigail, her mom, and her brother got in the car to head home, Mom said something interesting.

“You know, Abigail, you initially thought Sara was mean and didn’t want to play with you. You didn’t know anything about her and rushed to find a negative reason. I know you’re just learning, but we need to be careful not to judge people so quickly until we get to know them,” Mom said.

“You’re so right, Mom,” Abigail said. “Thanks. I think I felt kind of hurt by her ignoring me, and my hurt changed into anger.”

“That is understandable,” said her mom.

Abigail and Sara played together almost every day at the park. Day by day, Abigail learned more sign language, and Sara became better at reading lips. The girls became best friends, and thanks to Sara, Abigail grew up to become a sign language translator, helping kids and people who can’t hear!

A Special Message For You

Have you ever been too quick to decide if someone was good or bad? Maybe there's a new kid at ballet class that sometimes steps on your toes? She may just have a harder time getting the rhythm and getting her feet to move the right way. I bet she's trying her best.

Or what if you were in the library and saw a boy reading a book without letters? You might think he was weird if you didn't understand that he might be reading Braille. Kids who are blind learn to read with tiny dots on the page. It's super interesting! They learn which dots make up which word and use their fingers to read the stories. Or maybe you went to a new restaurant and saw something like a fun skate ramp next to the stairs. Did you know it's not just a fun way to get to the door, but it's a ramp so that a kid with a wheelchair can enter the restaurant, too?

All of us are born with many abilities, but some may not have the same abilities as you. Some of those differences may be easy to see at first, and some may not, like Sara's. But really, that different kid is still just a kid who wants to have fun, play games, and share with others too. They also deserve and need love and kindness like you.

Abigail wants you to follow her magic advice—don't be so quick to judge others without getting to know them. You may find out you actually have a lot in common—like you both really love butterflies!

SANTIAGO'S SECRET LANGUAGE

Meet Santiago! He's from Mexico and loves spending weekends at home with his big family. His grandparents live with him, so his aunts, uncles, and cousins often come over to visit. Yes, it is a *really* big family, and Santiago's house is always busy with him, his two sisters, and three cousins running around playing so many different games.

But dinner time is everyone's favorite time because Santiago's grandma, 'Abuela' as the kids call her, makes the yummiest soup, Pozole; a traditional dish she used to make in Mexico.

Santiago loved weekends for one more reason—he could speak Spanish, the language he was most comfortable speaking, all weekend long. You see, outside his home, Santiago only spoke English at school and with friends. Almost nobody knew that Santiago could speak Spanish. And because he didn't want anyone to think he was different, he tried super hard to be like everyone else.

Apart from awesome weekends with his cousins, Santiago's next favorite thing to do was Cub Scouts. He had been a scout for a year now and always looked forward to anything his troop would do. So can you imagine how excited he was when it was announced that their next adventure would be camping? Overnight! *I'll miss my family on the weekend, but I feel like the luckiest kid ever to go camping overnight!*

Finally, the big day came. As the troop climbed onto the bus that would take them to the campground, Santiago waved goodbye to his mom.

"Bye, Mom!" Santiago exclaimed.

"Have fun!" his mom said, waving back.

Santiago couldn't wait to get to the campground and enjoy a new adventure.

"Alright, everyone. Are you excited for this weekend?" asked the den leader, Mr. Smith.

“Yes!” all the boys squealed with excitement.

The campground was two hours away, so the boys kept busy with camp songs, jokes, riddles, and Santiago’s favorite—trivia questions.

Once they arrived, they had a one-hour hike through the reserve to their camping site. Once there, everyone did their part to help, and in no time, all the tents were pitched, firewood was collected, and they were all ready for their first skills training session.

Mr. Smith gathered all the boys and announced their first assignment.

“Scouts, we’ll be doing orienteering. That means you will read and navigate your way around using only a map and your compass,” Mr. Smith said.

Santiago and the boys were super excited. The group took their maps and compasses and headed off.

After about twenty minutes of exploring off the track, they heard someone cry out in the distance.

“What was that?” Liam said.

“I’m not sure,” said Mr. Smith. “It sounds like someone’s in trouble. Let’s see if we can help.”

Still using the map to track their movements, the troop headed in the direction of the sound. As the scouts got closer, they heard a “Help! HELP!”

They all followed the voice and finally came across a man and his son. Oh, no! The little boy had tripped and slid down a slope off the edge of the path!

The panicking dad began speaking and explaining what had happened so fast, but no one in the troop could understand him.

"He's not speaking English!" cried Tommy, who began shaking at the sight.

As Mr. Smith pulled out his phone to see if he had enough cellphone reception to use a translation app, Santiago froze. He understood every word the man had said because it was in Spanish. Santiago was filled with fear, not only for the boy stuck down the slope but also for himself. He had an important decision to make. *If I do the right thing and help the father, I will reveal my secret language. What will people think?* Santiago thought. *I've worked so hard to fit in so that no one thinks I'm different!*

But Santiago was a good kid, and he knew what he needed to do. He stepped up from behind the group of scouts, took a deep breath, and spoke to the man, "Estará bien. Estamos aquí para ayudar!"

Everyone stopped talking, and Mr. Smith lowered his hand from holding his phone high in the air.

"Santiago! Do you understand him?" he asked.

"Yes, Sir, he's speaking Spanish," and for the first time, Santiago said, "I'm from Mexico, and I speak Spanish too."

Then Tommy interrupted, "You speak Spanish?! Why didn't we know that? What did you just tell him?"

"I told him everything would be okay and that we are here to help," Santiago said.

"Hey, how come you never told us you could speak another language?" Tommy asked.

"Well, how about we discuss that later, boys? Right now, we must help this family," Mr. Smith said.

Santiago began translating between the father and the troop, and soon, they coordinated the best way to rescue the boy.

Once the boy was safe in his dad's hands, the family thanked Santiago and his troop in Spanish.

As they headed back to the campsite, Santiago explained to the group all about his big family coming from Mexico, the fun they had together, and, of course, his favorite soup.

"But Santiago," said Liam, "why haven't you ever told us this? Your life sounds so fun!"

"Really?" Santiago was surprised.

"Yeah!" said Tommy. "You are so lucky to speak two languages! That's what saved this boy! And the food your Grandma makes sounds so yummy!"

"You're so cool!" laughed Liam.

"Wow, guys, I thought if you knew I was different, you wouldn't like me or think I was weird or something," Santiago said.

"No way!" the boys exclaimed.

"Well, you guys are great. Other people might think I'm weird," Santiago said.

"Well, that should be their problem, not yours!" Tommy said.

Just then, Mr. Smith joined in. "You know Santiago, Tommy is right. You shouldn't be ashamed to show people the real you and all of you. Those who know and care about you will support you no matter where you are from or what other languages you speak. I'm very proud of you for stepping up when it mattered. You shouldn't see your differences as a weakness but as a strength. Your unique talents and background can serve those around you as they did today!" he said.

"Thanks, Mr. Smith. I've never thought about it that way," Santiago replied.

"Hey Santiago," said Liam, "you know how your background can serve us again today?"

"How, Liam?" Santiago asked.

"Please tell us you know how to make your grandma's soup. I'd much rather have that than the simple noodles we have on the fire now!" Liam said.

Everyone burst out laughing.

"I wish I did," said Santiago.

That night, the boys made smores at the campfire. Of course, they did. It's not camping without smores! They told more jokes, and it was the perfect ending to a great day. But to Santiago, the day was even more special; he didn't only help save that boy today; he saved himself the most by just being, well ... himself.

A Special Message For You

Do you have any hidden talents that you are afraid to share? Do you think you are different and that it is a bad thing? Do you also speak languages that others do not know, or are you from a country they've never heard of?

Maybe you have a pet lizard you haven't mentioned to your friends because no one else has one, and you think you might be teased about it. How about changing the way you think? Wouldn't it be cool to let your friends touch your unique pet? Maybe they will get a lizard too, and your lizards can become friends! Or, if you are from somewhere different, wouldn't your friends think it's awesome if you could tell them stories of faraway lands they have never been to? You may be hiding some of the most interesting parts about yourself. Wouldn't you be amazed to discover that the girl who always sits in front of you has a dad who is an astronaut, or that the boy you play soccer with can snowboard too?

Santiago wants you to see your differences as something interesting and unique that you can share with others. So, the next time you hear someone speaking a different language, it might be cool to know which one it is. Did you know there are more than 7,000 languages in the world? Now isn't that totally amazing?!

THINK MORE KIDS SHOULD READ THIS BOOK ?

It's through your support and review that my book is able to reach the hands of more children. Please scan the QR Code below to leave a review, or just simply click a star-rating for this book. It all helps!

(If you reside in a country that isn't listed, please use the link provided in your Amazon order.)

3 Simple Steps!

1. Open your camera on your phone
2. Hover it over the QR code below
3. Rate or review this book

.com

.co.uk

.ca

It only takes 60 seconds to make a difference. Thank-you!

HASIKA'S HENNA HANDS

Hasika was happier than usual lately. Why? Because it was her favorite time of the year—Diwali, the festival of lights! It's the biggest and most important holiday in her Hindu religion when people light lamps outside their homes to celebrate the victory of good winning over bad, and light being stronger than darkness. It's a beautiful thing to celebrate, don't you think?

Hasika and her family started preparing for the exciting festival a few days before. There was so much to do! They decorated their home with little clay oil lamps called 'diyas' and created colorful circle patterns all over the floor using colored powders and sand. Hasika loved designing the red, orange, and yellow circles. Haskia's family dressed in their fanciest clothes for the big day, and, of course, a delicious feast—pistachio barfi, cheese dumplings, cardamom biscuits, crispy and spicy samosas, rice pudding, carrot halwa, and many other treats were waiting for them. Yum!

But to Hasika, the best part of the whole festival was getting her hands decorated with henna designs.

"I can't wait to get my hands tattooed!" Hasika cheered.

Of course, it isn't a real tattoo that stays forever. Henna designs are drawn on the skin using a special paste made from the dry leaves of a henna tree. The paste is red-brown and only lasts a few days. It's an old tradition and very important for Hindu women, including Hasika and her sisters.

Finally, Hasika had her henna hand design! It was so pretty, with flowers and circular patterns stretching all over her hands, from the top of her fingers to her wrists.

"Wow!" Hasika shouted when she saw her hands so beautifully decorated.

Her sisters loved their henna designs too. They showed their hands to each other and smiled happily. "Look at mine!" said Hasika.

Hasika had the best day with her family, but one thing made her even happier—when all the fun of the festival was over, her beautiful henna design was still there! She could show it to her friends from school!

I'm sure everyone will like it and wish they had it done too! Hasika thought.

The day after the Diwali celebrations, Hasika couldn't wait to go to her classmate's birthday party with her design still on her hands. *Perfect for a party!* She thought.

She was just so excited to share something so important to her culture with her friends.

However, their reaction wasn't what Hasika had expected.

"Hey, look at Hasika's hands!" said one boy.

"Thanks. It's..." Hasika began but was immediately interrupted.

"They look dirty! Didn't you take a bath?!" said a girl.

"No, no, they aren't dirty! It's..." Hasika said.

"Go wash your hands!" Another girl said.

Hasika was so embarrassed and hurt. She couldn't understand her friends' words. Something so beautiful and important for her was simply funny and dirty to them.

She looked again at her hands and took a deep breath. With her eyes full of tears, Hasika sat at the picnic table, all alone, and waited for the time to leave.

Suddenly, a group of girls walked over to Hasika.

"Can we see your hands?" asked one of them.

At first, Hasika wasn't sure what to do. *Are they going to make fun of me, too?* she wondered.

Hasika looked at the girl, whose smile seemed sweet. She slowly moved her hand and stretched her fingers in the air.

"Wow!" the girl exclaimed. "How beautiful! Hey, girls, check out these fantastic flower patterns!"

"How cool!" a second girl exclaimed.

Hasika couldn't believe it. A big smile appeared on her face when she heard those words.

"Thanks," Hasika finally said.

"Is that a tattoo?" the girl asked.

"Well, not really," Hasika replied. "It's a henna design, but some people call them henna tattoos. We use parts of the henna plant to make the paint, and that's why it's red-brown. But it only lasts for a few days. It's an old Hindu tradition to celebrate the festival of lights," Hasika explained.

"The festival of lights? What's that?" one of the girls asked.

"It's Hindu's most important holiday, just like Christmas for some people," Hasika said. "We celebrated yesterday."

"Oh, I had no idea. I've never heard of it," the girl said.

The other kids heard them chatting and realized how wrong they were about calling her hands dirty.

"Oh, Hasika, I'm really sorry," said the boy who made fun of her. "I didn't know about it."

"I'm sorry too," the girl said.

"Me too," repeated the kids who had teased Hasika.

"Thank you," Hasika said.

Hasika felt much better hearing everyone say sorry for their teasing. She realized that she was the only Hindu girl in her class, and her friends really didn't know anything about her religion and traditions. They had never seen henna hands before.

"Lucky you! I wish I could have such a beautiful design!" said another girl.

"Well, I could draw it on your hand, but I don't have henna paint with me," Hasika said.

"But maybe we can find something else to use?" the girl said.

One of the girls found a washable marker and gave it to Hasika.

"Great! That will work!" Hasika exclaimed.

"But can you draw such beautiful patterns?!" the girl asked.

"Of course, I've done it many times before. I drew the designs on my sisters' hands too!" Hasika said.

Hasika took the marker and started drawing on her friend's hand. First, she drew a flower, then some round shapes similar to raindrops, and then some wavy lines stretching all over her hand down to the wrist.

"Wow! How amazing!" the girl exclaimed. "Thanks, Hasika!"

"How cool!" another girl said. "Please, I want to have the same one too!"

Hasika started drawing a similar pattern on her other friend's hand, adding some cute hearts too.

Soon all the girls were waiting in line to get their own! They all wanted to have their hands looking just like Hasika's!

Hasika was so happy and didn't stop drawing until all the kids got them! Her friends were so happy and showed their beautiful hand designs to their parents, who also learned something new about the Hindu religion.

In a few days, Hasika's beautiful henna faded, but its memory sure didn't. The following year, the kids remembered the festival of lights when they again saw Hasika's hands all decorated, and, just as before, they asked her to design their hands too! And they all had so much fun!

Hasika felt proud of her henna hands.

From then on, the Diwali festival was even more important for Hasika because it was her own victory of good over bad. From misunderstanding to understanding. After all, her friends finally accepted her diversity instead of making fun of it.

A Special Message For You

Do you know anyone who celebrates traditions in different ways? Have they shared things you didn't know about? Maybe you've seen Hindu diyas lighting up someone's front yard like Hasika's, or you've seen a Chinese dragon costume dancing to celebrate their Lunar New Year. Perhaps you decorate your Christmas tree while your Jewish neighbor sets up their Hannuka candles? People celebrate different cultures, religions, and traditions differently, each in its own special way. The people we meet can come from so many diverse backgrounds. It's not nice to tease or make fun because something or somebody is different. Try learning something new to understand! What you learn may actually brighten your day.

And if you are the one being teased, remember that sometimes people are afraid of what they do not know, and their reaction may show up as teasing. So why not explain the reason for the difference? Things will likely get better when they understand; you already know they are curious.

Hasika has a magic trick for you—no matter what religion you are or what tradition you have, be proud of it because it's part of you. And remember, be kind because others are proud of theirs too.

FINNLEY'S BLENDED FAMILY

"I'm so bored!" said Paul. And no wonder—it had rained every day that week, and he couldn't go out to play. Paul *loved* being outside. He looked sadly through the window at his wet and muddy backyard.

Oh, I wish I could go out! Paul thought.

But then, finally, that weekend, the sun shone through his bedroom window.

“Yay!” shouted Paul. He couldn’t wait to do something fun with his brother and sister.

“So, kids, what shall we do today?” Dad asked.

“The beach. The beach!” shouted Paul’s sister, Kimmy.

“Yes!” both Paul and his brother Jonah agreed.

“Beach it is!” said Mom, happy that all the kids were in agreement.

With everything packed in the car, the family was off to the beach.

“Woo hoo!” the kids cheered when Dad started the car.

The drive seemed to take forever, and when the family arrived at the beach, the kids ran out of the car, grinning, ready for whatever adventure the beach would bring.

Paul and Kimmy were off splashing in the water while little Jonah was busy building “The biggest sandcastle ever!”

“Hey, Mom! Look! Look how tall it is!” Jonah shouted above the sound of the rolling waves.

But it was hot, and soon the kids needed a break in the shade under their sun umbrella. There they sipped cool lemonade and ate fresh watermelon.

“What should we do next?” asked Kimmy. Before they could decide, Paul saw his friend, Finnley, from school, not far down the beach.

“Mom, can I go to say hi?" Paul asked.

"Yes, of course," Mom replied.

Paul ran over to Finnley with a big smile.

"Hey Finnley! You're here too! It's a perfect beach day, isn't it?" Paul said happily.

"It really is! I'm here with my family. Hey, come and meet them," Finnley said.

Chatting and laughing, Finnley took Paul over to meet his family.

"Mom, this is my friend from school, Paul," Finnley said. "And Paul, this is my little brother Leon and my stepsister Elena."

Finnley's family was friendly. They smiled and shook hands with Paul. They seemed so happy to meet him. Paul was glad to meet them, too. But still, he was a bit confused about the word 'stepsister.' However, he just smiled and kept chatting with the family.

Then a tall, kind-looking man joined them.

"Paul, this is my stepdad," Finnley said.

"Hey, Paul! Nice to meet you," said Finnley's stepdad.

"Hi!" Paul replied, even more confused.

"Did you bring a boogie board, Paul?" Finnley asked.

"I sure did! I'll go grab it," Paul said and rushed back to his family.

Paul couldn't stop thinking about Finnley's family.

"How's your friend?" asked Mom.

"He's good, Mom. He's also got a boogie board!" replied Paul. "Can I go and play with him over there?"

"Sure, okay. I can see you from here," said Mom.

"Mom... I was just wondering. What's a stepdad? I just met all of Finnley's family, and he's got a stepdad and a stepsister!"

"Oh, Sweetie, that just means he has a second dad. He has the dad he was born to and also his stepdad. You see, some parents don't stay married, and one of them might marry a new person, and that new person becomes the stepdad or stepmom," Mom explained.

"Oh, I get it, and the sister that came with his stepdad is called the stepsister?" Paul asked.

"Yes, pretty much. Families can come together in many different ways," Mom said.

"Oh good! I'm glad Finnley has a sister now, just like me. Okay, Mom, gotta go!" Paul said as he ran off to meet Finnley.

"Hey, I'm ready! Let's go!" Paul said.

Finnley ran to the sea with his boogie board, and to Paul's great surprise, Finnley's stepdad joined them too! The three of them had so much fun! They rode the waves, laughed, and sometimes even fell off the boards. And Finnley's stepdad was always looking out for them.

I can't believe Finnley's stepdad is so amazing—he's just like a real dad!

After almost half an hour in the water, they went out to take a break, and Finnley's stepdad bought ice cream for everyone! Yum!

The day at the beach was fun for all the wonderful parents and families. When they got home, the kids were tired and went straight to bed after another yummy treat: pizza!

Lucky for everyone, the next morning was Sunday. The kids were ready to make plans for another great day with their family.

"Mom! Dad! Let's go to the beach again!" shouted Kimmy.

"Not today, Honey," replied Mom. "Did you forget we're going to your Aunt Jenny's birthday party? She won't want us to miss it."

"Me neither! Aunt Jenny has the biggest pool! Let's go!" Paul cheered.

And yes, Aunt Jenny's big pool meant a big party with a lot of food, dessert, and more kids to play with. Soon, Paul and Jonah were splashing about with the boys in the pool.

But not Kimmy.

"It's not fair, Mom!" said Kimmy. "There are so many boys here for Paul and Jonah to play with and only one girl for me!"

"Well, Honey, you only need one! I bet you two might even have more fun than all the boys. Why don't you go over and say hi? Maybe she likes mermaids too," said Mom.

"Okay, Mom, I'm on it!" Kimmy said.

Kimmy raced to the girl with her mermaid doll in her hand. "I love your doll!" said Izzy, the little girl who looked just the same age as Kimmy. "Come check out my mermaids!" she said. And sure enough, those girls played nonstop with their mermaids for two hours.

Then Izzy's mom told her it was time to leave. Kimmy was surprised to see Izzy's mom, who didn't look like Izzy at all.

"Mommy, Mommy!" said Kimmy after she'd said goodbye to Izzy. "Izzy has to leave, but I think she's going with the wrong mommy! We need to help her!"

"Oh, Kimmy, it's okay. That's her right Mommy. I met her inside earlier. She's such a nice lady," said Mom.

"But... I don't understand. My friends' mommies look like them, and I look like you, but Izzy doesn't look like that lady at all!" Kimmy said.

"That's because Izzy was *adopted*. That means that for some reason, she can't be with the mom she was born to, but instead, she gets a new mom that loves her and will take care of her," Mom explained.

"Okay, Mom! I'm glad she gets to be with the nice lady, then. She did look so happy to leave with her," Kimmy said.

"Yes, Kimmy, just like Finnley's family, families can come together in different ways, but as long as there is love and happiness, they are lucky to have each other. Just as I'm so lucky to have you to love so much!" Mom said.

As Mom held Kimmy in a big, warm hug, she realized how glad she was to begin sharing with her kids the idea that families can come in all sorts of amazing packages. And Paul, Kimmy, and Jonah were happy to learn the magic ingredient that makes a family—love!

A Special Message For You

Have you noticed your friends might have families that are different than yours?

There may even be differences in your family. Some kids live with just their dad, while some may live with just their mom and may or may not see the other parent on the weekends. Maybe you know a friend who lives with his grandparents? Or your neighbor lives in two houses, half the time at her mom's house and half at her dad's.

Finnley wants you to remember that every family is different, but they all should have the same ingredients: love, kindness, happiness, and acceptance. There is no one right type of family, but the best is the one where you feel loved and safe—no matter how your family comes together.

FOTINA'S FAVORITE FOODS

Fotina was up super early, and her heart was beating so fast. Can you guess why? It was her birthday! Fotina wanted to have a big party with all her friends. She decorated her home with balloons and colorful ribbons, and her mom made yummy food—all Fotina's favorite dishes and desserts! Finally, everything was ready, and her friends would be coming any minute!

While she waited, Fotina hugged her mom, “Thanks, Mom! My friends will be so happy!”

As her friends arrived one by one, everyone became more and more excited. After wishing Fotina a happy birthday, they raced off to play party games, open presents, and sing songs. It was all so much fun! It was a perfect party, except for one thing.

Even though the table was covered with so many delicious things to eat, barely anyone touched the food.

Then, as the party went on, the kids began complaining that they were hungry.

“Hey, kids, you can eat the yummy food from the table whenever you like,” Fotina’s mom reminded them.

Yet still, hardly anyone touched it. At first, Fotina’s mom was confused, but then she realized that although she had prepared Fotina’s favorites, the other kids might not be familiar with their national Greek foods.

So, she happily explained each dish and invited everyone to try it.

But not one person wanted to. Instead, the kids begin to ask, “Where is the pizza? When is the pizza coming?”

Not understanding why this was happening, Fotina replied, “We aren’t getting pizza today. My mom made all this yummy food for us. These are my favorite Greek foods! You’ll love it!”

But the kids just looked at the table and frowned.

"We want pizza! It's not a real birthday party if you don't have pizza!" said one girl.

Her friends' reactions to the food made Fotina so sad.

But her mom wanted the party to be perfect, so she went ahead and ordered the pizza.

The kids raced to the table and grabbed slices of the pizza as soon as they arrived. They continued playing after all the pizza had disappeared and had a great time.

But Fotina wasn't happy.

When all the guests left, Fotina asked, "Mom, why didn't they want the food? These are my favorites, and I was so happy to share them for the first time! No one even tried my delicious baklava."

"Well, Honey, people are sometimes afraid of things they do not know," said Mom. Especially kids when it comes to food.

"But Mom, it would be so much more fun if everyone was interested in everyone else and liked to try new things from different places," Fotina said.

"Yes, Honey, it would be," Mom said.

"Mom, the world is full of so many different foods to try, and new adventures are everywhere!" Fotina said.

"I know. But not everyone feels the same, and some people are more fearful of differences than others. Don't worry, Honey, I know everyone still had a lot of fun at your party, and the bouncy castle was a winner!" Mom said.

That night, Mom got to thinking about what Fotina had said. It would be nice if everyone had the chance and was willing to try different foods. Suddenly, a light bulb went off in her head, and she had the best idea!

The following day, Fotina's mom shared her idea at the community center where she worked, and everyone loved it. Soon word had spread about the community center's 1st Annual Cultural Food Festival!

Anyone in the area could sign up to showcase their favorite family dishes of their culture and share samples so that others had the chance to try them. Many people signed up, all wanting to share, taste, and enjoy traditional foods from many countries and cultures. The event was going to be spectacular.

At school, the news about the event was buzzing, and Fotina was so excited and so proud that it was her mom who had organized it. A few other families from her class were also joining in, and those who weren't bringing food began to get curious about the excitement.

"Amy, will you be going?" Fotina asked her friend.

"Um... I don't know... There is nothing special about the food we eat at my house. My favorites are just regular pizza and mac n cheese," Amy said.

"Well, those are yummy, too, for sure. But wouldn't you want to get a glimpse of what other homes may be cooking?" Fotina asked.

"Well, I guess that could be interesting," Amy said.

“Then that's it. I hope to see you on Sunday!” Fotina exclaimed.

Sunday morning, the community center was filled with many different smells and colors as people displayed their native flags. The hall was buzzing with excitement as those sharing food set up their displays. In the middle of the hall, there were lots of tables and chairs for people to sit and eat the foods they wanted to try.

Fotina and her family set up their table, too, of course. They had brought many of the same foods that Fotina had at her birthday party: mousaka, souvlaki, Greek salad, and, of course, baklava for dessert.

“Amy!” Fotina suddenly shouted. “You’re here!”

As Amy looked at Fotina’s display table, she recognized some of the food from the birthday party.

“Are these the same as at your party?’ she asked.

"They are! Please, will you try this one here?" Fotina said, holding up a delicious dessert. "I helped make this one. It's baklava, and it's super sweet!"

"Yes, please," Amy said.

As Amy bit into the sticky, sweet layers of pastry, her eyes popped wide open.

"Fotina, this is the most amazing thing I ever tasted!!" Amy exclaimed.

Fotina laughed, "Told ya it was awesome!"

Of course, Amy and her mom tried all the different foods on Fotina's table.

"Why didn't I try these at your party?!" Amy said. "I'm sorry..."

"It's okay; the great thing is that you're trying it now," Fotina said. "And maybe you can walk around and try lots more."

"Definitely!" said Amy's mom. "Thank you for being a part of this."

The rest of the day went well, and soon all the displays were out of food. The 1st Annual Cultural Food Festival was a success, and plans for the second one next year were already being discussed.

The next year, it wasn't only the festival that was a success. At Fotina's next birthday party, everyone was willing to try all the new food. Although it was Amy who ate most of the baklava!

A Special Message For You

How do you react when you see a new food? Maybe it's something your mom brings home or something you see at a shop or restaurant. Maybe it's the lunch your friend's dad sends him to school with. Do you know that there are so many diverse foods in the world? Even several versions of the same thing.

Just think—spaghetti might come with a red tomato sauce or with a white creamy sauce, and that changes the flavor. Or how about even simple chicken? Would you like to have baked chicken, stewed chicken, fried chicken, curry chicken, roasted chicken, barbecue chicken, or sauteed chicken? I can go on, but you get the picture. Often, the type of food cooked in someone's home has been influenced by what that family ate hundreds of years before. And hundreds of years before that, those people ate the type of food that was available where they lived. Now, over the years, with travel, the internet, and people around the world getting to know each other, ideas and recipes for cooking get swapped, and new things are created. Isn't this just fascinating?

Follow Fotina's magic trick. Why not try something different by someone different and learn all you can about how and why that food was made? Don't waste those tastebuds on just a few things. Let your taste buds have a new food party as often as possible!

MASON'S UNIQUE MIND

Jett was up early this morning, as most kids are when something exciting is happening. Today Jett was going on vacation to a beautiful lake with his family. All his cousins would be there too, including his favorite cousin, Mason, who was the same age as him.

"Yay!" Jett cheered when he first heard the news about the vacation together.

Jett packed his favorite toys and games to play with Mason. They'd had so much fun playing together since they were little boys. Jett was especially excited to bring his new favorite board game because the two of them had never played this one together before.

Mason is going to love it! Jett thought while he packed the game at the top of his bag so he could easily get it out right away.

As soon as the family arrived at the lake, Jett unzipped his bag, took out his board game, and called out to Mason. "Mason! I've got a new board game to show you!" Jett didn't want to go swimming first or even enjoy a delicious ice cream! All he wanted was to play this game with his favorite cousin, Mason.

"Jett, look. Your cousins are building a sand castle!" Mom said. "You love playing in the sand. Do you want to join them first? There's plenty of time for the board game."

"No, thanks, Mom! I want to stay here and play with Mason," Jett replied.

Since he couldn't wait to start playing, Jett quickly told Mason all the rules of how to play the board game. It wasn't a difficult game, but still, there were some rules to follow.

"See, this is where you start. You'll play with the red piece, and I'll take the blue one," Jett explained. "Do you get it?"

"Well, I guess..." Mason said.

"It's easy, you'll see! Let's start!" Jett said.

The boys were so happy to be playing together again, but soon things were not so fun. It seemed that Mason hadn't understood the rules completely.

"No, Mason, that's not right," Jett said, feeling frustrated.

Mason tried again.

"You're doing it all wrong!" Jett shouted. "Didn't you listen to the rules?! Focus on the game!"

The boys continued without Jett explaining the rules again.

Jett just wanted to play, not waste more time going through boring rules.

But, of course, the same thing happened again—Mason made a mistake while playing the new game since he didn't fully understand the rules.

Jett was so angry that he couldn't control his temper. He couldn't understand how Mason didn't get such an easy game. He just wanted to have fun!

"I can't believe it! I told you the rules!" Jett shouted and walked away to sulk alone under the shadow of a tree.

Mason was happy the game was over. It wasn't fun at all for him.

He joined his other cousins playing in the sand.

Jett got even angrier seeing Mason playing happily with the others.

He went to his mom, his eyebrows scrunched up angrily.

"What's wrong, Sweetie?" asked Jett's mom.

"I don't want to play with Mason ever again! He isn't my favorite cousin anymore!" Jett shouted.

"Why? What happened?" asked his mom.

"Why can't he get the game, Mom? I told him the rules! He's not a baby! We are the same age!" Jett complained.

"Well, some kids learn differently," his mom said. "He may take a little longer, but it's not his fault. You know, he's not doing it on purpose to upset you."

"But why, Mom? Why can't he just get it like me?" Jett asked.

"Everyone is born differently and with different skills. Some kids have a knack for getting the hang of ball games, and some find board games easier, and that's why each person is uniquely special. Mason is different than you in how fast he can learn something, just like you are different than your sister in how fast you can run," Mom explained.

"Oh... I didn't think of it like that," Jett said.

"Now that you understand, are you still angry with him?" Mom asked.

"No, Mom, I feel bad for yelling at him. I'm happy he even wanted to try the new game with me because I think he really wanted to go straight to the sand. I should remember that just because I have fun with someone doesn't mean they do all things the same way I do," Jett said.

"That's my boy!" Mom said.

"Thanks, Mom!" Jett said, his scrunched-up eyebrows smoothing out. "Can I go now? I want to go have fun with my cousins!"

"Of course, Sweetie," Mom said. "Have fun!"

Jett rushed off to join his cousins playing in the sand. But when he arrived, he heard arguing and shouting. One of his cousins was yelling at Mason.

"You destroyed our sand castle! What's wrong with you?! Can't you do anything right?" The cousin shouted.

"Hey, leave him alone!" Jett said. "It's not his fault! Why don't you show him how to do it instead of just yelling at him?"

"Thanks, Jett..." Mason said.

"Come, Mason, let's go and play with my new board game," Jett said.

“But I don’t know how to play it,” Mason said.

“Don’t worry about that. I’ll explain the rules again, and it’s okay if you don’t get it at first,” Jett said.

Jett and Mason sat under the tree with the board game. Jett explained the rules to Mason again, and the boys started playing. Mason made some mistakes again, but this time, Jett didn’t lose his patience. Each time Mason made a mistake, Jett gently showed him the right thing to do. After a few more mistakes and a few more times of Jett showing him again, Mason understood the rules, and the boys started to have a lot of fun with it.

Jett won twice, and Mason won three times in a row!

The boys spent the whole afternoon playing Jett’s favorite board game. And you know what? It became Mason’s favorite board game too!

That day, Jett learned an important lesson about diversity. He realized that no one was exactly like him. There are things he may be better at and things others may be better at. Understanding that keeps Jett from getting too upset when people do things differently than him. From then on, when something did not make sense to Jett, he tried to think about why or even ask why. Knowledge gained from understanding differences had a positive impact on how he treated people in the future.

Jett grew up to become a teacher working with kids with special needs in learning. And, of course, Mason is still his favorite cousin!

A Special Message For You

Do you have a friend who learns slower than you, or maybe a friend who speaks differently because he stutters? Or are you maybe the one with a tendency to daydream the most, and you're often asked to pay attention more?

We don't all have the same brains or minds, and we may learn things at different paces or even in different ways. Some people learn a topic better with pictures; some learn better by hearing about it, while others may prefer reading about it. No speed or way is wrong or right; it's just their unique way. But no matter the differences, we can all have something that's the same: a kind heart.

Jett has a magic trick for you—if you happen to know or meet someone who learns a bit slower than you or keeps getting things wrong, instead of getting mad, try to understand their needs and help if you can. Jett knows it will mean a whole lot to them.

HADIA'S HIJAB HELP

Something big had just happened to Hadia. Her family had just moved to a new country! Hadia, a chatty and friendly eight-year-old girl who easily made friends, was scared of being around people for the first time. She was used to easily making lots of friends, but with kids who were all like her—they ate the same food, played the same games, and, most importantly, dressed the same way.

Hadia knew that most people in the world didn't dress like the people in the country where she was born. And now she was about to start a school where all the kids were dressed so differently. One thing about her clothing bothered her the most—the hijab.

The hijab is a traditional covering that covers the heads of the Muslim women and girls in her hometown. But here, not many people wore them. Hadia was worried that most people probably wouldn't know how normal it is where she is from.

What will they think of me? I bet they have no idea why I even wear it. Will they let me be friends with them? Hadia wondered.

As Hadia stepped out of her mom's car at the school gate, her tummy filled with butterflies. She could immediately feel the stares and confused looks and hear the passing whispers.

"Don't worry. It will be fine," her mother said. "You'll get through these first days and make a nice friend soon."

Hadia took a deep breath, held her head high, and walked through the gate, down the hallways, and into her classroom.

Safe at last, she thought. *I'm sure my classmates will be kind to me now that I'm in the classroom.*

But that's not what really happened. Instead of stares that Hadia could walk past, she was now an easy target sitting at her desk. The comments and questions began.

“What is that on your head? Why are you wearing it? Can I touch it? Do you sleep with that? What color is your hair? Do you have hair under that?” her classmates questioned, one after the other.

To Hadia’s relief, her new teacher, Ms. Martin, walked in, and the questions stopped.

"Okay, class, settle down. As you all seem to have noticed, we have a new student. This is Hadia. Hadia and her wonderful family moved here two weeks ago, and we are happy to have her,” Ms. Martin said.

“Thank you, Ms. Martin,” said Hadia.

But Ms. Martin noticed the confused faces in her class and the many side glances at Hadia. She knew she might need to answer the questions of some curious students, so she thought of a plan very quickly.

“Okay, class, today we are going to begin discussing cultures and religions around the world. It’s quite an exciting topic, as there are so many differences to be celebrated across many countries. In honor of our new classmate, let's start there,” Ms. Martin said. “Hadia, where is your family from originally?”

“Indonesia,” she replied.

“Wonderful, let’s take a closer look at your country,” said Ms. Martin, and she pointed to Indonesia on the map. Then, it was easy to direct her discussion to the traditional clothes worn in that country.

On the large digital smart board, Ms. Martin showed the class photos of some women and children living in Indonesia dressed in traditional clothing. It was so different from anything the kids had ever seen before. And it was so different from their usual headwear, such as hats, visors, or baseball caps.

Just seeing the photos of her homeland gave Hadia a feeling of comfort.

"You see, kids, the hijab is a head covering, like a head scarf, that many Muslim women and girls wear as part of their religion. They come in many beautiful colors and styles," Ms. Martin explained.

"Wow, they are beautiful!" said one girl.

"'What colors do you have, Hadia?" asked another girl.

"I like the light pink and the light purple ones," Hadia replied. She was so excited about the questions she was now receiving from her classmates.

"As you can see, kids, for you, Hadia's hijab might be a new thing, but to Hadia, she is used to seeing it all the time. Now that you know more, do you have any other questions for Hadia?"

"Yes! Can I touch it?" Jackie asked.

"Well, only with her permission," Ms. Martin said.

"Hadia, can I touch your hijab?" asked Jackie.

“Yes! And anyone else, too! I want you all to feel comfortable with me,” Hadia happily exclaimed.

The kids asked Hadia a few more questions that she was glad to answer.

Soon, the bell rang for lunch, and Hadia and her new friends headed to the cafeteria. But once again, Hadia could feel the stares from the other kids who didn’t know her.

“Why are you wearing a large napkin on your head?” one child, Roly, shouted as he held up a cafeteria napkin on his head, teasing her.

But just as Hadia was about to hang her head in embarrassment, her classmate Billy stood up.

“It’s not a napkin, Roly! It's called a hijab!” Billy said.

Hadia looked up.

“Well, it's still weird,” replied Roly.

Now, all the students were watching. Then Jackie stood up, too.

“It’s not weird. It’s very normal where she’s from! Just because it’s different doesn’t mean you can make fun of it,” Jackie said.

As harsh as Roly’s words were, it was very comforting to Hadia to hear her classmates defending her.

With nothing more to say, Roly sat down. Hadia’s classmates, Billy and Jackie, sat next to her.

“Just ignore him,” Billy said.

“Yeah, he knows nothing about it!” Jackie added.

“Thanks, guys,” Hadia said, and lunch time continued as normal.

And just as her mom had said, each day was easier than the one before. No one ever teased Hadia after what happened in the cafeteria, and the stares slowly went away, too, as people got used to seeing Hadia and as she made more friends who understood her.

Over time, the kids learned many new things about Hadia’s culture and traditions. Some kids even visited Indonesia with their parents on summer vacation as they wanted to see Hadia’s country and some of the sights they’d learned about. At the same time, Hadia got to know the traditions of her classmates, which were new to her. Sharing experiences and learning new things was so exciting and useful for all of them.

A Special Message For You

Have you ever seen a girl or a woman wearing a hijab on the street or maybe on TV? Has it seemed strange to you? Have you ever wondered why they wear them? Even if you haven't seen it, I bet you won't be bothered by it now that you know more about it!

With the chance to travel to so many different places in the world, people no longer need to stay in their countries, cities, or villages. And when they travel, they may still carry lots of their customs from their homeland. You may see different types of dresses, headwear, hairstyles, and maybe even different footwear. We are so lucky to get to meet all kinds of people from all kinds of places. And traditions we once only read of in books, we can see in our neighborhoods, malls, or maybe just passing us by in the airport.

Hadia wants you to remember something—nothing is weird or silly; it's just different and maybe even super interesting! With so much information on just about everything, be curious, ask questions, and get to know this whole wide, wonderful, and interesting world. Hadia says that even if people look different on the outside, on the inside, we are all still the same. We all smile when happy, cry when sad, and we can all wave to say a friendly hello!

MINATO'S MIGHTY MUSIC

"Minato loved music so much. Ever since he could remember, he had always wanted to be a drummer in a music band with his friends.

Back when Minato lived in Japan, he played an instrument that was very special to him: the traditional Japanese Taiko drum. “It makes the best sound ever!” Minato would tell his friends, who knew the taiko well. But since he moved to America, he hadn’t met anyone else who played the Taiko drum, and he felt a bit strange talking about this instrument to his new friends.

Soon, Minato was no longer interested in playing his traditional drums. He found other musical instruments to play that were more common in America. He played the trombone and completely gave up playing what was once his favorite instrument.

One day, when Minato came home from school, there was some exciting news. His great-grandmother in Japan was turning 100 years old, and all the family was going over for a big party! You can imagine how important that birthday would be. Minato was about to burst with excitement—his first visit to Japan since he'd moved away!

Minato loved being back in Japan. The very next day was the super special birthday party. There were so many people there! Cousins, aunts, and uncles—it felt like he'd never left. His great-grandmother's house hadn't changed either, with the same little pond in the garden. Minato remembered how his cousins used to pretend to go fishing there, though they dared not actually catch any of her shimmering orange and white fish.

Music filled the air, and there were traditional decorations everywhere. And then Minato heard the familiar sound that made him stop in his tracks. The biggest smile spread across his face.

Could it be? Minato thought, his heart pumping fast.

Yes, it is! The sound of the traditional taiko drumming, DOM, DO-DOM, DOM, DO-DOM, thumped from Minato's great-grandma's front lawn.

People began to make their way out to the front of the house as a full taiko group was playing. This was it! This was Minato's favorite instrument in the whole world—the one he'd enjoyed playing so much.

Listening to the beloved sound, Minato couldn't resist asking if he could join the group and play. His heart was full while playing it, and all the good feelings and love for the instrument flowed naturally from his heart, down through his hands, and onto the drum.

"Oh, my dear Minato! Thank you!" his great-grandmother said. "Hearing you play is the best present I could get for my birthday!"

Minato hugged his great-grandmother, and tears of joy poured down his cheeks.

On the plane ride back to America, all Minatoa could think of was drumming that amazing Taiko drum. When he got home, before unpacking his bags, Minato rushed to the garage. Can you guess what he was doing? Yes, he was dusting off his taiko drum and drumsticks. "I'm going to start playing again, Mom!" he shouted. "And play every day!"

And he did. And he completely forgot about the trombone.

Two weeks later, his teacher announced that the school was having a talent show, and anyone who wanted to participate could join. Minato's mind immediately went to his taiko drum, but the exciting thought only lasted a moment.

Oh, I can't play the taiko drum in front of everyone. They won't understand like they do in Japan. They'll think it's boring. They might even tease me! he thought. *Maybe I can just do something with my trombone.*

But whenever Minato thought about the talent show, he could only picture himself playing the taiko drums. Struggling with his fears, he went to his dad for advice.

"Dad, what should I do? I really want to play my taiko drum at the talent show, but the kids might think it's weird. What if everyone laughs at me?" Minato said.

"Minato, don't be worried about showing who you really are. Taiko drumming is a part of your culture, and you shouldn't be ashamed of it. Japanese culture is and will always be a part of you. It's a part you should be proud to share. Plus, you're so good at it, and you love it! The kids will be happy to hear you playing because your love of it will shine through," his dad said.

"I think you might be right. Thanks, Dad," Minato said, and he hugged him tightly.

The following day at school, Minato signed up for the talent show. "Taiko drumming," he wrote down next to his name. He practiced and practiced day after day. He wanted to show his friends his very best effort.

Soon, it was showtime, and Minato was ready. With his drum on stage and bravely facing his fears, Minato introduced himself and shared a little about his instrument and why it is so special to Japanese people.

“You probably haven’t seen an instrument like this before. It’s a taiko drum, and it has been a part of Japanese culture for thousands of years. It is used in religious ceremonies and festivals, like celebrating a new harvest. Long ago, it was used in battles to cheer the soldiers, and the army used it to talk to each other,” Minato explained. “I just love the sound of it!”

The entire hall was silent as Minato's hands began to tap the drum. Most of the audience had never heard such a sound and were so excited that they listened carefully.

At the end of his performance, the audience was on their feet. The kids clapped their hands, cheered, and chatted with each other. They were so happy to hear a completely new sound.

“Congrats, Minato!” said one of his friends.

“That sounded so cool!” said another.

“Thanks, guys!” Minato happily replied.

Minato was so proud that he'd followed his heart and faced his fear of people perhaps not liking something they did not know about.

At school the next Monday, Mianto's class began clapping for him when he arrived. Minato was a star! They were amazed by his unique performance. Minato couldn't be happier.

And guess what happened at recess? Two brothers, Jenji and Tomo, came up to Minato and thanked him for helping them see that they didn't need to be afraid or ashamed for liking an instrument that no one knew. Yes! They were also from Japan and used to play the taiko drums, too! This was the best reward for Mianto's bravery. He found friends to play taiko drums with!

Even better, Minato and his new friends made a band! The boys performed together at the school talent show every year and at other events in their town.

They continued playing together even when they grew up and finished school. The boys now have a famous taiko drum school, and they get to teach and share their love for Taiko with many others. Now, isn't that a dream come true?!

A Special Message For You

Is there something that you like doing but think others will not like? Do you really want to join a jazz dancing class or maybe even hip-hop dancing, but wonder what your ballet dancing friends will think?

Or maybe your talent is magic tricks, but you think your friends will laugh at you if the trick goes wrong? Maybe you also have a traditional instrument from a different country that you want to play again. Is it the steel pan from Trinidad and Tobago or the kantele from Finland? Try an internet search in your community to find a group of people already playing the instrument you like, or maybe even start your own group. Just because something isn't popular doesn't mean you can't do it. People are filled with so many diverse talents. It would be sad if no one could see you shine. Would a music band of 100 flutes be more exciting than a band of ten or more different instruments? It's the same with life!

Minato wants you to remember his magic trick: be brave, follow your heart, and let your differences shine! Your differences and your unique talents are exactly what the world wants more of.

SAMMY'S IMPORTANT SATURDAYS

Samual, who preferred to be called Sammy, loved video games so much. He could tell you *everything* about all the latest games. And no, he wasn't stuck in front of the game all day. He loved to read everything about his favorite games, too.

Sammy's friend Oliver, who lived next door, loved playing video games with him on Wednesdays after homework. Every Wednesday, Oliver rang Sammy's doorbell at exactly 5 pm. You could time your watch on it! They had one hour to play as much as they wanted.

"I've learned *so* much from you, Sammy. I'm so lucky to have you as my gaming buddy," Oliver said.

But one Wednesday, Oliver couldn't wait to see Sammy and rang the bell at 4:45 pm.

"Hey Oliver, you're fifteen minutes early. How come?" Sammy asked.

"Sammy, I just couldn't wait to tell you the good news!" Oliver exclaimed.

"Oh, tell me!" Sammy said.

"We are going to enter our first-ever video game tournament! Can you believe it?!" Oliver said.

Sammy jumped up in excitement. With his eyes and mouth wide open, he couldn't believe what he'd just heard.

"What? Are you kidding me? How is that happening?" Sammy asked.

"They are setting it up at the community center! Anyone can sign up!" Oliver exclaimed.

"Awesome!" Sammy said, high-fiving his friend.

"We have to practice so much today. It's going to be next Saturday, so it's only ten days away!" Oliver said. "I know we can win!"

Suddenly, Sammy hung his head, and his smile disappeared. Oliver was confused to see this sudden change on Sammy's face. This wasn't the reaction he expected.

Any other day except Saturday would be perfect! thought Sammy, *Why did it have to be Saturday?!*

"What's wrong, Sammy? Aren't you excited?" Oliver asked.

"Well, I was when you first told me about it, but I can't do the tournament on Saturday," Sammy said sadly.

"Why not? What's wrong with Saturday?" asked Oliver, now completely confused. "Are you busy doing something else? What could be more important than the tournament?!" asked Oliver.

Sammy took a deep breath. Oliver knew that his friend Sammy was Jewish, but he forgot that Saturday was a holy day for Sammy's family. "Sorry, Oliver, but Saturday is the Sabbath. You know how strict my family is about that," Sammy said.

"But Sammy, lots of other Jewish kids get to play video games on Saturdays. How come you can't?" Oliver said.

"Yeah, Oliver, I know, but not all Jeweish homes are the same. There are different types of traditions that people follow. We are Orthodox Jews, and it's just the way we do it. I'm sorry," Sammy said.

"Well, who am I going to play with? Your religion isn't fair!" Oliver shouted before stomping out of Sammy's house.

Sammy felt sad. *How could he be so mean?* thought Sammy. Poor Sammy couldn't take part in the video game tournament, and now his friend was mad at him.

"Hey Oliver, back so soon from Sammy's today?" asked his dad, surprised. Sammy had never returned home a minute before that hour was up. "Was Sammy as excited as you about the video game tournament?"

"I don't want to talk about it, Dad. I'm too mad. Can I go to my room for a while?" Oliver said.

"Sure, buddy," Dad said. "If you want, we can talk about it when you feel a bit better."

"Thanks, Dad," Oliver said, and he walked to his room.

Oliver stayed there all afternoon. He couldn't stop thinking about the video game tournament and Sammy, who had let him down, leaving him without a partner at the video game tournament!

That evening, after dinner, Oliver told his dad he was ready to talk.

"Sammy can't be my partner for the video game tournament on Saturday because of his religion," Oliver said. "It's so unfair, Dad! I don't even get the idea of no electronics on Saturdays anyway!"

"Well, Oliver, Sammy's family sees the Sabbath as a day of rest, and these are their rules. You should accept that as a part of who Sammy is and respect it," his dad said.

"But why can't Sammy play video games on Saturday, but some other Jewish kids can?" Oliver asked.

"Almost all kids don't choose their religion or the rules. They are born into a family that believes in certain things, and they learn those ways from their parents just as their parents help them learn to walk and talk. People also have different celebrations based on those beliefs," Dad said.

"You mean, like how we celebrate Christmas, but Sammy's family does Hanukkah?" Oliver asked.

"That's right, you're starting to understand this better. Each religion has its own set of things they believe. Once kids get older, they may be able to decide if they want to keep up with that religion and beliefs or stop following, but until then, they respect their family's choices, and so must we. Just as you would want someone to respect your belief to celebrate Christmas, right?" Dad explained.

Oliver's mood suddenly changed.

"I guess I was only thinking about myself and the tournament," Oliver said with a frown. "I said some things that weren't nice. I will say sorry to Sammy tomorrow."

"That's my boy! I'm proud of you for understanding that differences like these should be respected," Dad said.

The next day, Oliver rushed over to see Sammy after school.

"I'm so sorry for what I said, Sammy!" Oliver said. "It wasn't fair at all!"

"It's okay, don't worry," Sammy said. "I wish I could play with you!"

"Me too..." Oliver said.

"I've got an idea! Why don't you sign up with Matthew for the tournament? I heard in school today that he doesn't have a partner either," Sammy suggested.

"Oh, thanks! I had no idea Matthew played video games! I'll ask him right away!" Oliver exclaimed.

Oliver was no longer angry, and with his calm mind, he was able to find a solution to his problem. He partnered with Matthew, and together they did quite well! They didn't win, but Oliver wasn't too sad. He rushed to tell Sammy all about the tournament.

Oliver and Sammy continued playing video games every Wednesday, having the best time together. Then you know what?

Something great happened! The next video game tournament was on a Sunday, and the dynamic duo was able to compete together. And... they won!

A Special Message For You

Does your family have a religion? Are there some things you may have to do that you don't particularly like, but then you get to have some pretty nice celebrations along the way too that you love? What other religions do you know about?

Maybe you are Muslim and celebrate an, or perhaps you're Hindu and get to have fun with the lights of Diwali. Or maybe you are like Sammy and celebrate Hanukkah, or are like Oliver and celebrate Christmas. Isn't it amazing that all these religions, plus so many more, exist in our world? And remember that some people and families choose not to follow any religion, and their choice should also be respected.

Sammy wants you to remember something—if you come across a religion or a tradition you haven't heard of before, why not look it up or ask someone about it? There is so much more to learn about the beauty and diversity of our amazing world!

SKYLAR'S UNUSUAL SUMMER

After two long months of summer vacation, all the kids had happy grins as they entered their classrooms. They couldn't wait to see each other again! Some had got braces, some new glasses, some had stories of summer adventures to tell, and some got taller. Many were just the same as they were before the vacation. Skylar, like the rest of her classmates, couldn't wait to see everyone again, but she was a bit worried too.

Something had happened to Skylar over the summer, and her looks changed a lot. She was hoping no one would notice, but then it came.

“Hey Skylar, what’s up with your new haircut? You look like a boy!” Jerry laughed.

“Yeah, Skylar, will you be using the boy’s bathroom today?" joked Lamar.

Skylar could also hear some girls whispering, “Why did she cut it so short? I would never cut my hair like that!”

Skylar tried not to notice or care. She knew this might happen, and so she walked into the classroom today, ready to be extra brave. But no matter how brave she was, those mean words still hurt.

In PE class, Skylar was having trouble keeping up with everyone and stopping to catch her breath often.

“What’s the matter, Skylar? Did you eat snail pies this summer?” said Lamar.

“Try to keep up, snail!” shouted Jerry.

I won’t let them bother me, Skylar whispered to herself.

The next day wasn’t much better. Skylar felt tired all morning, and Ben and Linda made fun of her when she almost fell asleep at her desk. As the bell rang and Skylar got up to leave, her legs felt weak, and she stumbled near her desk.

“Are you okay?” asked Ms. Wilson.

"Yes, I'm fine," Skylar said quietly.

But she wasn't fine.

Just before school closed last year, Skylar had gotten some bad news: She was sick. Over the holidays, while most other kids were running in the playground and building sandcastles at the beach, Skylar visited doctors, had lots of testing done, and took lots of medicine. Two of the side effects of her medicine were losing some hair and feeling super tired.

Being back at school was tough. The next day, Skylar wasn't feeling well enough to go to school, so she stayed home for some much-needed rest. Later that evening, she heard a ring at the door. It was Tracey from her class.

"Hey, Skylar, how are you feeling?" Tracey asked.

"Um... much better, thanks," Skylar replied.

"Are you sure?" Tracey pushed.

"Yes, yes, I am," Skylar repeated.

"Okay, but before I go, can you tell me what happened to your hair? It's not like you to want to cut your hair so short." Tracey said. "I feel like something else is going on."

“Thanks for asking,” Skylar said. “You are right about my hair.”

Skylar went on to tell her about her sickness and how she began to lose her hair.

“But it's growing back now, so I’m glad. It’s just short at the moment,” Skylar said.

“Well, I think it looks good on you. And don’t worry about those mean boys. If they knew why, they would stop,” Tracey said.

“Well, that’s the thing; people don’t really know what someone is going through, so they really shouldn't tease or bully at all,” Skylar said.

“That’s so true! Thanks for telling me. I hope you feel well enough for school tomorrow,” Tracey said.

As Tracey left, she thought more about what Skylar had said. She remembered last year when Suzy used to sit by herself on the bench and not play with anyone. No one knew then that her pet had died, but people made fun of her for being boring. And when Zelda didn't turn up to her birthday party, Tracey refused to talk to her for a week, but later, she found out that Zelda was on her way to the party but got in a car accident. She felt bad about that because she realized it wasn't Zelda's fault at all. But then Tracey remembered something else and had a brilliant idea. *I'll try to do it tomorrow!* she thought happily.

Tracey was so happy to see Skylar back in school the next day.

"How are you feeling?" Tracey whispered to Skylar.

"Good! Thanks!" Skylar replied.

As everyone got up and walked to the cafeteria, Jerry began teasing Skylar about her hair again. Tracey saw her opportunity.

"Hey, Jerry, do you remember when we were in kindergarten and we all had to work on a project about the planets using the different size balls the teacher had given us?" Tracey asked.

"Yeah," Jerry said.

"And do you remember you were the only one who came to school without your project and how we all laughed at you and called you a dummy for not knowing how to do it?" Tracey continued.

"Yes, I do. You guys made me cry so much," Jerry said.

"We only later found out that your brother had destroyed your project. But I'm sure our teasing didn't make you feel good," Tracey said.

"It didn't!" Jerry said.

"So if you felt that way, how do you think you make other people feel when you tease them?" Tracey asked.

"Not so good," Jerry said, hanging his head.

"Exactly! We don't always know what other people have going on with them, so we shouldn't judge or make fun of them. They could be going through something really tough!" Tracey said and sat down in her seat, very happy that she had hopefully made a positive difference.

And she did! Jerry never teased Skylar about her hair again. What's more, he never teased anyone again. And many other classmates learned a lot from Tracey that day.

When she was ready, Skylar shared her illness with her class, and Jerry and Lamar were very sorry for all that they said. Skylar realized that she was relieved to share her situation with her classmates; hiding it was so hard! Plus, the class had learned about an illness they didn't know about. They learned that it was not Skylar's choice to have short hair, and they also learned about ways to help girls like Skylar with their hair.

At the end of the class year, the girls prepared a special surprise for Skylar. They each decided to grow their hair long so that they could all cut it and donate it to places that make wigs for other children who temporarily lose their hair. Can you imagine how special that made Skylar feel?

A Special Message For You

When we see our friends at school, other kids at a park, or strangers in the supermarket, we really can't tell who's having a bad day or who may be dealing with something difficult in their home. A hurtful comment may make the situation worse. That's one reason we should be careful of the things we say to others.

But if we stick to positive words and kind comments, we can be sure we won't hurt anyone's feelings or make their day any worse. We may even make it a little bit better and be the cheer-up that they really needed. Yep, we just don't know for sure about the things happening in another person's life, so it's better to be nice. Maybe they lost something, like Suzy, or maybe they aren't feeling well, like Skylar, or perhaps an accident happened, like with Jerry's planets. If you notice something out of the ordinary with a friend, be gentle with their feelings. You can ask if they are okay, and even a sweet smile might brighten their day. We should all try to have positive effects on other people, so think about the words you're about to say before you say them. Will it be helpful or hurtful?

Skylar wants you to remember that one easy way to test your words is to see if you'd like someone else to say those same words to you. If not, don't say it. Isn't that super easy? And remember, everyone's situation may be different, so just treat people the way you would want to be treated.

VICTOR'S TASTY VEGGIES

It was the last day of school, and the class was full of chatter and laughter. But it wasn't just the great feeling of it being the end of school—their teacher, Ms. Taylor, had organized a fun treat—a pizza party! While munching on their pizza, the children chatted about their summer plans and also the great end-of-year barbeque that their classmate Joe was hosting. Oh yes, everyone was invited, and it would be epic!

Ring! Ring! Ring! The school bell rang, and it was the start of the summer holidays! The kids excitedly waved goodbye to Ms. Taylor. "See you tomorrow!" they said, high-fiving each other as they thought about the party the next day.

One by one, everyone arrived at Joe's barbeque party, happy and excited.

"Wow, I love the decorations!" said Mariel as she got to the party.

"Look at those huge balloons!" shouted Grayson, pointing up at them.

"Hey Victor, did you see those cupcakes on the table? They look awesome! I hope we can have them soon!" said Joe as he helped his mom hand out cups of lemonade.

While the barbeque was warming up, there were lots of games set up for the kids to play—a small volleyball court in the corner, a ring toss, and a bouncy house next to the huge pile of hula hoops. The kids ran from one corner to another, trying new activities and having lots of fun!

An hour into the party, everyone was starving, and Mr. Benson, Joe's dad, was just finishing the hamburger patties, hot dogs, and barbeque ribs on the grill.

Soon, he called out, "Come and get it!"

All the kids rushed over to the long picnic table for a yummy party lunch. As they sat down, the mouthwatering smell of barbeque made them even more hungry. Only one boy, Victor, left the table and walked over to Mr. Benson at the grill.

“Excuse me, Mr. Benson,” said Victor. “Do you have my vegetarian burgers ready, too?”

"Oh, Victor, I'm so sorry! Your mom did tell me, but I forgot to grill them. Silly me. Not to worry, Victor. I’ll be right back. I hope you can wait an extra ten minutes, and once again, I’m sorry for not remembering.”

“No problem, Mr. Benson. Thank you,” Victor said.

Victor headed back to the picnic table with his empty plate in hand.

“Hey Victor, what happened? You're not hungry?” asked Joe.

“Yeah, I am. I’m just waiting for my burgers,” Victor said.

“Your burgers? What do you mean? You are not eating with us?” Grayson said.

“Yes, I am, I... I...” Victor mumbled.

“What is it, Victor?” Grayson shouted.

“Well, I can't eat your burgers,” Victor mumbled.

“Our burgers?” Grayson asked. “And what’s wrong with our burgers?”

“Yes, your meat burgers. I can only eat vegetarian burgers,” Victor replied.

“You mean like veggie burgers?” Grayson asked.

“Kinda, but it tastes much better than it sounds,” Victor said.

“No way! Veggie burgers are just not real burgers! It’s like we are eating the cow, and you are eating the grass,” laughed Grayson.

"Oh, stop, Grayson! That's not nice,” said Mariel. “They aren't really made of grass, right, Victor?’

“Oh no, it's a mix of vegetables, grains, and things like beans and lentils,” Victor said.

“I bet it tastes like cardboard!” laughed Grayson again.

“Grayson!” shouted Mariel angrily.

“Well, he’s not completely wrong,” Victor said. “At first, I didn’t like them, but the people that make them have gotten so much better at making them taste almost like real meat burgers!”

Just then, Mr. Benson arrived. Having overheard some of the kids’ chatter, he added, “Victor is right. They do make them taste great now. There are also veggie nuggets, veggie corn dogs, and veggie meatballs.”

“Wow, Dad!” said Joe. “You know a lot about this, too!”

"Yes, Joe, these veggie alternatives are quite healthy to eat, and they give you a lot of energy. Do you remember those corn dogs you and your sister love to eat on Saturday mornings? Those are veggie!” Dad said.

“What? I can’t believe it! You never told me!” Joe exclaimed.

“If I did, would you have eaten them?” Dad smiled.

“Well, I guess not...” Joe replied.

“But don’t you love the taste of them?” Dad asked.

“Yeah! I love them!” Joe said.

Suddenly, someone else joined the conversation.

“Wow, I'm sorry for what I said, Victor,” said Grayson. “I’m curious! Mr. Benson, can I try one of Victor's burgers?!”

“Me too!” said Mariel.

Then, all of a sudden, all the kids wanted to try the veggie burgers, and Mr. Benson had to make a whole new batch.

“This is going to be fun. Plus, I get to tell my mom I ate veggies at the party!” laughed Grayson. “She’ll love that.”

Soon, the new burgers were ready, and just as you can guess, the kids couldn’t get enough of them.

As he stuffed the last bite into his mouth, Grayson offered some surprising words to his classmates.

“You see, guys, you shouldn’t speak badly about something if you haven't yet tried it. This is the best veggie party ever!” he exclaimed.

As everyone cheered with him, not only did Victor feel a sigh of relief, but he also felt happy that he could share something healthy with his friends.

“Mr. Benson!” called Victor. “Can we have some not-so-healthy but so-so-yummy cupcakes now?”

“Of course! Everyone, come and get 'em!” Mr. Benson exclaimed.

And just like that, everyone rushed to the table and finished off the delicious cupcakes.

At last, the party was over, and everyone said goodbye to Joe.

“Thanks, Joe!” they shouted as they headed home, grateful for fun, friends, and yummy food.

“Hey, Dad,” said Joe.

“Yes, Joe,” replied his dad.

“Can we buy some of those veggie meatballs you mentioned earlier? I’d like to try those too. But don’t tell Cindy it’s veggie yet. Let's keep the healthy secret to ourselves!” Joe said.

Dad chuckled, “Sure! We can tell your sister next year. Now, will you help me clean up this backyard?”

"Of course! Thanks for the party, Dad!" Joe said.

The following weekend, Joe had veggie meatballs for dinner. And yes, of course, he loved the taste of those too! He can't wait to tell Victor when school starts again.

A Special Message For You

Would you have made fun of Victor like Grayson? Or do you think you would've reacted more like Mariel, with curiosity?

It can be an easy first reaction to tease someone who does, eats, or says something that you're not used to. Instead, try thinking about why they have made the choice to do what they do and understand it. You might even want to try it yourself and have something new you can enjoy. Some things can sound weird at first, but once more and more people have tried that new thing, they begin to realize that the different thing is actually a good thing.

There are many different reasons why people might eat different foods. It could be because of their religion, like how some Muslims don't eat pork meat, or maybe it's a special diet they have to follow, like Victor. Or maybe someone has a food allergy, and eating certain foods can be very dangerous for them. Luckily, there are very yummy options for most people, like sugar-free gummy bears for those who can't have too much sugar and almond milk ice cream for those who can't have cow milk. Have you ever tried cauliflower rice, zucchini noodles, or pumpkin peanut butter cookies?

Victor wants you to be careful about being too fast to judge people for their food choices. And remember, just because someone is eating something different, that's not a reason to tease them. Keep an open mind about food, and be curious and adventurous. You never know what your next favorite lunch, dinner, or snack might be. Just ask Joe; he still eats those veggie corn dogs every weekend!

CONCLUSION

Hi there!

Thank you so much for reading this book.

Minato, Fotina, Sammy, and Victor hope you've enjoyed discovering the magic of diversity and uniqueness that is all around us.

This magic is part of what makes you so special and unique, too. Imagine if we all looked the same, talked the same, and liked only the same things. What a boring world!

Hasika and Hadia want you to be proud of your religion and traditions. They are so fascinating and beautiful in their own ways! Becky wants you to love your unique looks; everyone has a beauty of their own. Skylar wants you to be brave even when you're going through hard times, and Santiago wants you to proudly show off your unique skills and talents. Go out there and shine!

All these twelve new friends want you to embrace your uniqueness and be happy to share it with others!

Being unique and truly yourself in a world where many people try to fit in and copy each other is such a brave way to be. Your courage to be proud of being exactly who you are IS the true magic!

You can help this magic grow and spread around the world by sharing it with your friends and helping them accept and love themselves just the way they are. And don't forget to remember to respect and be kind to those who may be different than you in whatever way.

If you happen to feel the magic has stopped working, just go back and read the stories again. Your twelve diverse friends will be happy to see you and more than happy to remind you of how special you are and how wonderful our diverse world is.

And shhh, top secret! More of my inspiring stories are coming soon.

Until then,
Bye-bye!

WANT MORE STORIES?

Check out these two other books in our collection:

Inspiring Stories for Amazing Boys:

Captivating Tales to Build Self-Confidence, Cultivate Teamwork, Foster Kindness, and Encourage Brilliant Problem-Solving

Available on Amazon.
Scan here

Inspiring Stories for Amazing Girls:

Enriching Tales to Empower Self-Confidence, Build Strong Friendships, Comfortably Express Feelings, and Bravely Choose Kindness

Available on Amazon.
Scan here

It's through your support and review that my book is able to reach the hands of more children. Please scan the QR Code below to leave a review, or just simply click a star-rating for this book. It all helps!

(If you reside in a country that isn't listed, please use the link provided in your Amazon order.)

3 Simple Steps!

1. Open your camera on your phone
2. Hover it over the QR code below
3. Rate or review this book

.com

.co.uk

.ca

It only takes 60 seconds to make a difference. Thank-you!

The End

Made in United States
Troutdale, OR
12/11/2024

26258792R00066